ORP AND THE FBI

ORP AND THE FBI

Suzy Kline

G. P. PUTNAM'S SONS • NEW YORK

ACKNOWLEDGMENTS

Special appreciation to:

My editor, Anne O'Connell, who helped me with this manuscript.

Thank you for your criticism, questions, and hard work.

My husband, Rufus, who has read more mysteries than anyone I know.

Thanks for listening to me and reading the many versions of this manuscript.

Victor Hurtuk's brother Eric.

Thanks for sharing your fishhook experience with me.

And for Dashiell Hammett's *The Maltese Falcon* and his character Sam Spade.

Thank you for your inspiration.

G. P. Putnam's Sons, a division of The Putnam & Grosset Group, 200 Madison Avenue, New York, NY 10016. G. P. Putnam's Sons, Reg. U.S. Pat. & Tm. Off. Published simultaneously in Canada. Printed in the United States of America. Text set in Palatino. Interior artwork by Patrick Collins.

Library of Congress Cataloging-in-Publication Data

Kline, Suzy. Orp and the FBI / Suzy Kline. p. cm.

Summary: Twelve-year-old Orville and his friend Derrick form their own detective agency and, with help from Orville's younger sister Chloe, investigate the arrival of an unusual letter and the appearance of a mysterious intruder.

[1. Brothers and sisters—Fiction. 2. Friendship—Fiction. 3. Mystery and detective stories.] I. Title. PZ7.K6797Ou 1995 [Fic]—dc20 94-24552 CIP AC

ISBN 0-399-22664-8 10 9 8 7 6 5 4 3 2 1 First Impression

For my mother,
Martha Swihart Weaver,
with love

Thanks for helping me with this story,
and for the good times we had on our 1993 summer
trip to the Swihart Homestead
in South Whitley, Indiana.

Contents

MYS·TERY

1. anything that arouses curiosity because it is unexplained, or secret

2. a puzzling crime

3. something not understood, or beyond understanding

4. the behavior of someone given to secrecy or intrigue

5. something having a symbolic significance

syn – problem, enigma, riddle, puzzle, conundrum, obscurity

1
Bathtub Detective

"ORVIE!" my sister hollered into the bathroom. "You've been in there an hour now!"

Of course I was. I get my best ideas when I'm sitting in the tub.

Today was Monday, the first official day of spring break, and I was trying to come up with a list of exciting unsolved mysteries around the house.

Right now I had the window open for a cool April 2nd breeze, my size ten sneakers on the faucet handles, and a clipboard full of disappearances:

1. Ralph's dog dish
2. our TV knob
3. seven gym socks

Actually, I could care less about the missing socks, but finding some would enhance my standing with Mom. She's been in a bad mood lately.

4. Mom's cat earring

Might as well throw that one in, too. Mom's been complaining about it.

5. Uncle Gus's green basketball

Uncle Gus is my favorite relative. He taught me how to make a hook shot. At twenty-one, he was a junior college All-American basketball player.

Now he's thirty, a bachelor, and kind of crazy. I think his beard is neat and so is his messy apartment. He has his own gas station. It's called Gus Stasion's Gas Station. Gus's girlfriend is Trang Foo. If they ever got married, she'd be Trang Stasion.

Names are kind of weird in my family. Take mine, for instance.

ORP.

Those are my initials, for Orville Rudemeyer Pygenski. It's much easier to say and spell ORP than . . .

"ORVIE!"

Suddenly the door opened a few inches and I saw part of my sister's fat fifth-grade face. I hate it when she calls me Orvie.

When she saw I wasn't really taking a bath, she looked relieved. "I knew you were in your think tank."

"I don't know, Chloe. One of these days you might catch me in the buff."

"Buff?" she said. I could tell my word choice turned her off. During vacation Chloe is usually working on some great novel, so she's very choosy with her words.

"You mean nude, bare, undressed, unclothed, or unadorned?"

"I mean *naked as a jay.*" Then I flashed a big smile. It was great being two years older and wiser than my sister.

"Orvie, your voice is changing."

"Naturally!" I said, flexing my muscles. "Feast your eyes upon a *real man.*"

"Okay," Chloe said. Then she reached down

and pet my dog, Ralph, who was sleeping next to the tub.

I grabbed a damp washrag and hooked a shot at her. She caught it with her left hand as she stood up. "Have you seen my cinnamon-flavored dental floss? It's been missing for a week now."

"I'll add it to my list of unsolved mysteries."

Chloe turned around. "Is that what you're doing?"

"Yup. Derrick and I are opening up our own detective agency. We're sleeping in the tent tonight so we can start working on our first major case."

At this point, it looked like the missing basketball. But, Chloe didn't need to know that.

"Mom's letting you sleep outside?"

"I haven't asked yet."

"Good luck. So . . . you like mysteries?"

Chloe picked up her toothbrush and pointed it at me. "I've got two biggies for you."

"Whoa," I said. "Are they as thrilling as your missing dental floss?"

Chloe ignored my question. "Take a look outside."

"Where?"

"Next door."

Since I was mildly curious, I got up and looked out the bathroom window.

"What?" I said. There was the Kushman house. It was about ninety years old, had three stories if you counted the attic, and the living room had lots of windows.

"Do you know why all the drapes are closed?"

"Yeah. The Kushmans are in Florida for three weeks. Their house is empty."

"How do you know it's empty?" Chloe asked.

"What are you talking about?"

"For the past few nights at eight o'clock a dim light comes on in the living room and I can see a human shadow behind the curtains. It moves back and forth for about half an hour. See that big side window in the front?"

I looked where Chloe was pointing.

"That's where it appears."

"No kidding!"

Chloe put her toothbrush back in the holder. "No kidding. And another thing. Mom got a mysterious letter last week from someone named Greg Parks in Ohio."

I hated the way Chloe abruptly changed topics. I still wanted to talk about the eight o'clock shadow.

"Guess how I knew it was mysterious?"

I didn't guess because I was only half-listening. My eyeballs were still glued to the Kushman house.

"Because . . . after Mom read it, she ran to the mirror, stared at herself and started crying."

I turned around. "Mom was crying?" That was hard to picture. She doesn't do it very often. The last time was when she stepped on a sewing needle and had to go to the emergency room. But that was last summer.

"How did you know it was from Craig Parker?"

"Greg Parks," Chloe corrected. "I fished his blue envelope out of the garbage and read the return address."

"Who is he?"

"He lives in Ohio. That's all I know right now."

Chloe was a natural snoop.

"So," she continued, "if your detective agency needs some assistance, let me know. I have a good eye for unusual plots."

I thought about it.

Having my little sister in my detective agency was the last thing I wanted, but Derrick and I needed her cases.

Who cared about Ralph's missing dog dish anyway? Except Ralph.

No, "The Eight o'Clock Shadow" and "The Mysterious Letter" were the cases to crack.

"You're hired," I said, handing her the clipboard. "Derrick and I could use a good secretary."

"Secretary?" Chloe laughed. "No thanks. I was secretary in your 'I Hate My Name Club' last summer. Remember? I'm due for a promotion."

"How about my assistant?"

Chloe shook her head. "A full partner."

Boy, was my sister stubborn!

And bossy.

Well, there was *no way* she was going to butt into our FBI meetings. Those were *strictly* private.

Between Derrick and me.

I just had to use a little strategy.

"What about your novel? Don't you have writing to do?"

"I've got writer's block. I need some new experiences."

"Oh."

Chloe and her words.

Then I thought some more.

Words. . . .

Chloe loved them.

"Okay. You can be our . . . *consultant.*"

"Consultant?"

I could tell by the way she raised her eyebrows that she was impressed. She knew one at Cornell Middle School. It was Mrs. Buffington, the reading consultant. Chloe liked her.

"For whom am I a consultant?"

"My FBI."

"FBI?"

"Famous Bathtub Investigators."

Chloe's eyebrows dropped. "Bathtub?"

"Hey, the bathroom is the perfect office. It's where I do my best thinking and it's private."

"But it smells sometimes," Chloe groaned.

"How can it?" I said. "It doesn't have a nose."

"ORVIE!"

The King of Detectives

That night after dinner while Dad listened to the news and Mom went on an errand, I waited on the front porch for Derrick. When he arrived at 7:25, I hardly recognized him.

"I'm ready for our two cases," he said, standing under the porchlight. I had filled him in on the phone that afternoon.

I checked out his snap brim hat, vest, suit jacket, and tie. The only thing he had on that made sense was his pair of jeans and sneakers. "Who are you supposed to be?"

"Remember when we rented the video *The Maltese Falcon* last Saturday night?"

"Of course I do. That's what gave me the idea about starting our own detective agency."

"Well, Orp, after you loaned it to me Sunday, I studied Sam Spade all day. I love the way Humphrey Bogart plays him!"

When Derrick handed me the video, I was reminded who would be returning it. And who paid for it.

Me.

Derrick was the biggest tightwad at Cornell Middle School.

"So guess who I'm going to be for our school talent show next week."

"Sam Spade," I said.

"You got it! The King of Detectives! Listen to this, Orp!"

Derrick pulled his snap brim hat down over his forehead and made his voice grind like Humphrey Bogart. *"I know where I stand now. Sorry I got up on my hind legs, boys, but you fellows trying to rope me made me nervous. Miles getting dumped off upset me, and then you birds cracking foxy. But it's all right."*

I clapped. "Go, Derrick."

"Think I can beat Moses Malone's lip sync? He took first last year."

"Truth?" I said.

"Truth."

"Since the judges are teachers, they might go for it. Most of them like Dashiell Hammett who wrote the Sam Spade mysteries. The guys in the audience? That's another thing. Be prepared for boos. It's nerdy."

"Hey," Derrick shrugged, "like Sam Spade says, 'Those are the chances we take.' "

I liked Derrick's independent spirit. "What did you do? Memorize a whole scene from the movie?"

"Yup, *and* . . ." Derrick pulled a list from his inside pocket. "I carefully selected two dozen phrases. Each one is vintage Sam Spade."

I shook my head. He made a phrase sound like fine wine.

I always knew Derrick was a movie addict but this was going too far. He was going to be booed out of the place.

Then I thought about it some more. Derrick was always there for me when I played basketball or baseball. Movies was his thing, like sports was mine.

"Okay, Sam," I said. "Show me your list." Derrick handed it to me and I read it under the porchlight.

1. "A lot of dough"
2. "You're just stalling."
3. "In the cooler"
4. "I told you to keep her away from me."
5. "Bumped off"
6. "Think fast."
7. "Laid eyes on her"
8. "I won't play the sap."
9. "You've got brains."
10. "Those are the chances we take."
11. "I was walkin' around thinkin' things over."
12. "Want a drink, Angel?"
13. "Don't crowd me."
14. "Nose to the ground"
15. "Beat it."
16. "I won't squawk."
17. "Bum steer"
18. "Hit the hay."

19. "Take your paws off me."
20. "Schweetheart"
21. "Hot tip"
22. "Who put that bright idea in your head?"
23. "Got him right through the pump."
24. "PDQ"

"What's the last one?" I asked.

Derrick snapped his suspenders. "I didn't know that one, either. I had to check it out with the local police. The sergeant transferred me to the detective bureau. When I got a detective, he kind of laughed. He said they use those initials all the time. Then he acted like he didn't want to tell me what it meant."

"Did he?"

"He gave me the first and last words."

"Not the second?"

"No."

"What were the ones he gave you?"

"Pretty quick."

I smiled. "No biggie. We got it. What do you say we start our stakeout of the Kushman house? It's seven forty-five. Want to hit the lights?"

"I'll get them," Chloe said, stepping out onto

the front porch. "Sorry I'm late, boys, I was just finishing a chapter in a new book. Want to know the title?"

Derrick and I exchanged looks.

"Shadow in the Side Window."

"What is *she* doing here, Orp?" Derrick whispered.

"That was one detail I forgot to mention in our phone call today. Eh . . . Chloe is our FBI *consultant.*"

Derrick pulled his hat down over his eyes. I could tell he wasn't happy.

"Nice snap brim hat, Derrick. Where'd you get it?" Chloe asked.

Derrick's answer was in a monotone voice. "My granddad had it in our attic. He was a banker in the fifties."

I had to admit Chloe was good at getting information. I didn't think to ask about that.

"Let's squat over here, boys, on our front porch," she said. "That way we can spy over the railing and not be seen. It's a perfect view of the Kushmans' side window. We can look right across our driveway into their living room. There's enough light from the street corner so we won't stumble around."

"Don't crowd me, Schweetheart," Derrick snapped.

Score one for Dashiell Hammett!

Chloe lowered her eyebrows. "Don't tell me, Derrick! You're Sam Spade from *The Maltese Falcon*! I know, I just saw it Saturday night."

"How could you?" I said. "You were writing in your bedroom. Mom said Derrick and I could watch that by ourselves."

Chloe was quiet for a long time. I suspected she didn't mean to blurt out that piece of information.

"You were spying on us!" I snapped.

"Not really. Just the movie. Your conversation was boring."

Derrick and I groaned.

Chloe was looking more and more like the enemy. And here she was infiltrating our FBI with our consent!

Derrick whispered in my ear, "Can't you get rid of her? Come on, Orp. You've got brains. Think fast."

I started thinking as Chloe started lecturing.

"I hate Sam Spade. He was a sexist! He never called women by their real names. They were 'Dahling' or 'Precious' or 'Angel.' He treated women like they were rattlebrained. I'd never stand for that."

Suddenly it hit me.

If Derrick and I threw a lot of Spade lingo at her, maybe she'd be bugged enough to quit. I whispered the idea in Derrick's ear.

"Who put that bright idea in your head?" Derrick whispered.

We slapped each other a quiet five.

"Come on you guys," Chloe scolded. "No secrets. We're equal partners here."

"Uh-huh," Derrick and I hummed.

3
The Shadow

When I looked at my watch, I was glad it had a luminous dial. "It's seven fifty-seven. The Shadow will be appearing any minute now."

Derrick and I squatted and peered over our front porch railing. When Chloe put her hand on my shoulder, I seized the moment. "Take your paws off me!"

"Gee!" Chloe groaned.

Score one, I thought.

As we continued our surveillance of the Kushman house, we thought less about Chloe and more about the Shadow.

We kept our eyes peeled on the side window of the living room. The only thing in front of it was a trimmed cedar bush.

"So, Orp, when did the Kushmans leave?" Derrick asked.

"A week ago."

"When will they be back?"

"Two weeks."

"No one ever goes inside that house?"

"Nope," I said. "We pick up their mail every morning and keep it in a box in our kitchen."

"And you've seen the Shadow every night since they left?" Derrick asked.

"Uh-huh."

"Correction," Chloe replied. "*I* was the one who saw the Shadow each night."

"Right, Schweetheart."

"Orp, cut it out!"

Derrick and I winked at each other. It was working.

When I checked my watch again, it was 7:59. We didn't say one more word.

That was the longest minute I could remember. We kept our eyeballs on that big side window.

We didn't want to miss the appearance of the Shadow.

At exactly eight on the button, a dim light came on in the living room. "Whoa!" Derrick said as he checked his watch. "The Eight o'Clock Shadow *is* punctual!"

We watched the dark shadow move.

Back and forth.

Up and down.

Behind the drawn curtains in the living room.

"What's he doing?" I said.

"Beats me," Derrick said.

"Did you see that? A leg! I saw a leg in the air," Chloe pointed out.

"It's kicking something!" Derrick replied.

Suddenly we heard it.

A crashing noise.

And then we didn't see the Shadow anymore.

"Where'd he go?" I said.

The next five minutes seemed like an hour.

We waited.

No shadow.

Then the dim light went off.

I took out my notebook and scribbled a few notes in the dark.

At 8:22, we heard the Kushmans' back door open and close.

"Let's go!" I said.

We jumped over the railing and ran across our driveway that separated the Kushman house from ours. By the time we got to the Kushmans' back door, the Shadow was gone.

"He got away!" I groaned.

We stood there shaking our heads for a moment, then headed back to our house. Derrick stopped at the spigot and picked up the hose. After he turned on the water, he walked up to Chloe.

"Want a drink, Angel?"

"Don't call me that!" Chloe snapped.

I cracked up.

"I think we better have an FBI meeting in our office," I said.

Derrick guzzled some water from the hose. "I'm impressed, Orp. I didn't know we had an office. Where is it?"

"In the house."

"Okay," Derrick replied. "But I have to *go* first."

"No problem."

Our First FBI Meeting

After I clued Derrick in about our office, Chloe and I waited outside the bathroom.

A few minutes later, Derrick came out.

"Sorry," he said, closing the door behind him. "Maybe we should wait a minute or two before we go in."

"I told you this would happen," Chloe complained. "It's a dumb place for an office, Orp."

"Hey! We just have to let the air clear for a few minutes."

Chloe rolled her eyes.

Derrick made a victory sign with two fingers. He knew Chloe was close to the edge. "You know," he said, "in *The Maltese Falcon,* Spade and Archer had their names on their office window. We should put our names on ours."

"Good idea! I'll take care of that now." I went into the kitchen, got some paper, a Magic Marker, and tape.

When I got back, I opened the bathroom door and went over to the frosted window.

Quickly I taped our names on the glass.

Chloe came in, took one look, and complained. "ORP, DERRICK, and SCHWEETHEART! That's not funny!"

Derrick and I cracked up.

"Eweyee!" Chloe said. "It still smells in here! That's it! I'm starting my own agency."

Derrick and I put our thumbs up.

Chloe stomped out. A moment later she poked her head in the doorway. "I just thought of the perfect name for my detective agency."

"What?" we groaned.

"The CIA."

"CIA?"

"Chloe's Investigation Agency!"

"Good luck, Precious," I said.

"Ohhhhhhh you!" Chloe replied, slamming the bathroom door in my face.

Derrick and I had a good laugh as I crossed off the name Schweetheart on our office window.

At 8:33, we got serious.

It was time for our first FBI meeting. I got comfortable in the tub. Derrick sat down on the fluffy pink toilet seat and pulled up the wicker hamper for his feet.

"This isn't exactly like Sam Spade's leather chair that he leaned back in," Derrick complained.

"I know," I said. "There are a few drawbacks."

"What about the phone? Every detective agency has one."

"If we need one, I can bring the extension cord in here."

Derrick nodded. He remembered I talked to him lots of times from the tub.

"So what do we know about the Shadow?" Derrick began.

I took out my notebook. "The Shadow's punctual and destructive."

"The guy must have a key," Derrick said. "Do you think he's a family member we don't know about?"

"Maybe," I said. "But why so sneaky? Why

always at eight o'clock? And why just one light?"

Suddenly there was a knock at the door.

"ORVILLE?"

It was Mom. She was home from her errand. "What are you doing in the bathroom?"

Derrick got up, opened the door, and invited her in. "Please have my seat, Mrs. Pygenski."

I was impressed with Derrick's straightforward approach.

Mom looked surprised and dazed as she sat down on the toilet seat.

Then Dad appeared in the bathroom doorway. "You look pretty sharp, Derrick. This the new FBI headquarters, son?"

"Yeah. See our sign?"

"I saw both of them."

"Both?"

I jumped up and Derrick and I took a quick peek around the bathroom door.

FBI

(Fat Booger-eating Idiots)

Chloe!

And her CIA!

I ripped off the sign and crumpled it up.

"Yeah. We're having a meeting," I said, climbing back into the tub. Then I fired the ball of paper into the wastepaper basket.

"Two points," Dad chuckled. "I wondered what you kids were doing on the front porch."

Mom looked worried. "What?"

Before we could explain, Dad blurted out, "Haven't you heard of Boston Bull, dear? He's been on the evening news all week."

At that moment, Ralph strolled in. He seemed interested, too.

"Some guy escaped from Enfield Prison last week and has been hiding somewhere. He was last seen at the Country Hills Mall wearing a Chicago Bulls T-shirt and a Boston Red Sox cap. The reporters have since nicknamed him Boston Bull."

Derrick took off his hat and fiddled with the brim. "What was he in the cooler for?"

Vintage Spade, I thought.

"Armed robbery," Dad said. "He shot the bank teller in the foot."

"The teller was lucky," Derrick replied. "Some guys get it right through the pump."

Mom wasn't impressed with Derrick's tough-guy act. "Well, you kids stay around the house. Don't go wandering off somewhere in the dark looking for him."

Suddenly Chloe poked her head in the doorway. "Better stay in the yard, boys."

"OUT!" I yelled. Chloe was probably eavesdropping the whole time about Boston Bull.

Mom stood up. "Excuse me, but I have a little project to do in the attic."

"I didn't mean you, Mom," I said.

"I know. But the attic's a mess. I have to separate what we should keep and throw out."

I was disappointed Mom couldn't stay longer. Having visitors made our office seem more official.

"Let us know if you find someone hiding up there in a Red Sox cap," Dad teased.

Mom made a face and then left.

After Dad followed her out, Derrick made an observation. "What's got into your Mom? Ever since I laid eyes on her tonight, she's been in a foul mood."

"I think her foul mood has something to do with that mysterious letter she got from Greg Parks in Ohio."

Derrick nodded. He remembered our phone

conversation about it. "Well, Orp, we've got two tough cases to crack, and CIA competition."

"Yup," I said. "We're going to have to keep our ears to the ground."

"According to Spade, it's nose, Orp."

5

The Mysterious Letter

When the phone rang at 9:02, I took the call in our office. Derrick was disappointed it wasn't for us.

"Oh, hi, Uncle Gus. Yeah, she's upstairs in the attic. I'll go get her."

I left the receiver in the tub and ran to the top of the attic stairs. "MOM . . . PHONE!"

I noticed she was sitting in the middle of the floor, looking at a pile of books. "Be there in a minute."

As soon as Mom came downstairs and started talking with her brother, I motioned to Derrick to go upstairs with me.

We were on the attic scene in seconds.

"Let's check on Mom's little project. I have a hunch it might have something to do with that Mysterious Letter."

When we got to the pile of books, I reached down and picked up the one on top. It was opened to a certain page. "This has got to be part of the puzzle!"

Derrick glanced over my shoulder. "It's your mom's high school yearbook from Ohio."

"And *this* is Mom's senior picture. There she is, twenty years ago!"

"Whoa," Derrick said. "She was a babe."

When I heard a faint laugh, I turned around. Chloe was sitting in the corner of the attic on our old footlocker.

Derrick and I ignored the CIA spy. We just looked closer at the picture. Mom was about twenty pounds lighter, and her hair twenty inches longer.

Chloe talked to us from across the attic. "Did you know Mom was the Belle of her class?"

I lied. "I knew long ago. Don't you think I'd be curious where I got my good looks?"

After Chloe choked, Derrick flipped through the pages about clubs.

"This is the one I want to join when I get to high school," he said. "The FBLA."

I read what the letters stood for: Future Business Leaders of America.

"That figures, Derrick. You want to be a banker when you grow up." I knew he always had to be the banker when we played Monopoly.

"Just like my granddad! I'm good at saving money."

"Yeah," I grumbled. I knew why, too. Derrick always let other people pay for things.

Suddenly Derrick turned the yearbook around and pointed to the lower corner.

We read the small print silently. We didn't want to share our information with the CIA.

Dear Margie,
When you smile at me, I melt like butter. I wish I was Orville and you were my girlfriend.
Love, Greg Parks

GREG PARKS!

Derrick and I immediately exchanged looks. He was the guy from Ohio who sent the Mysterious Letter!

Chloe hopped off the footlocker and walked over to us.

"Close the book, PDQ!" I said. "The CIA is coming."

Derrick did.

"What's PDQ?" Chloe asked.

"Any detective knows that," Derrick said. "Your CIA is slipping."

Just then Mom came up the attic steps. "What are you doing up here?" she asked.

"Looking for . . . " I panicked. My mind went blank.

"Your turn to think fast, Derrick!" I whispered.

"Eh . . . we were getting the tent," Derrick said.

"Tent? You want to sleep in the backyard?" Mom said.

"Yeah!" I replied.

"I don't know." Mom hesitated. "Spring nights can get awfully cold. Isn't it too early to sleep outside?"

Chloe seized the opportunity to get back at us.

"I'd say it was too late. It's after nine. How can you see what you're doing in the dark?"

I shot a look at Chloe. She made it seem like I had two mothers.

I held up a lantern. "We'll see just fine."

Derrick nodded. "That baby will flood the whole backyard with light."

When Mom hesitated, I knew I had her. I just needed the magic phrase. "I promise we'll put everything back neatly."

Chloe rolled her eyes.

"All right, boys," Mom said. "But be sure to take some extra blankets."

"We will. Thanks, Mom."

As soon as we got to the backyard, we turned on the lantern and got busy putting up the tent. Derrick could tell I was upset. I didn't say anything.

I thought about things, though.

Everytime I pounded a nail, I pretended it was Greg Parks. BAM! WHAM!

Derrick tried to divert my attention.

"Just look at all these dead mosquitoes, gnats, and moths, Orp! There must be hundreds of them cooked at the bottom of this lantern."

"Not now, Derrick. I feel burnt myself." I went over and sat on the picnic table and looked up at the stars. They lit up the sky like sparklers. I loved writing with those things in the night air. If I had one now, I'd write . . .

. . . and put a big heart around it.

Derrick joined me at the table. For a while we just inhaled the clean, cold air.

Finally, Derrick brought the painful subject up. "Do you think your mom is involved in a love triangle?"

"She better not be. I'd like my parents to stay married."

"Mine didn't," Derrick said, flipping his collar up. "It's not so bad, really. I see Dad every weekend. I'm used to it now."

I couldn't say anything more. The thought of my parents getting a divorce depressed me.

Derrick pointed to a plane's flashing red lights in the sky. Then he continued his analysis.

"I think your dad needs to give your mom more attention. This Greg Parks guy is probably coming to town on business and wants to see your mom. She's sad about not looking the way she used to and . . ."

Suddenly, there was a shrill scream from the attic.

Derrick and I took a flying leap off the picnic table and ran into the house.

6

Our Casework Gets a Snag

As soon as we got to the attic, we could see Dad, Chloe, and Ralph gathered around Mom. She was on her knees, holding a fishing pole.

"WHAT HAPPENED?" I yelled.

Mom's eyes were closed and she was gritting her teeth. "It's . . . in . . . my . . . back."

We looked behind her.

There it was.

A fishhook. The barbs had gone through her white T-shirt and inside her skin.

"What were you trying to do?" Dad asked.

"I . . . was practicing fly . . . fishing. And . . . I caught . . . myself."

Mom was one of a kind.

Dad cracked up. "You're the biggest catch of the season, dear."

"It's not funny, Orville. It's . . . very painful."

"I'm sorry, Margie," Dad replied. Then he kissed her cheek. "I know we have a high ceiling, but don't you think you should do your fly-fishing in the backyard?"

"Don't lecture me now," Mom snapped.

I looked over Chloe's shoulder. She was writing in her notebook. I could see what it was. A question: Why was she fly-fishing?

Chloe was amazing. She was continuing her investigation even during an emergency like this.

Mom winced when she let Dad help her up. "Where are you taking me?"

"To the emergency room," Dad replied. "I'm not pulling that barb out."

Mom put her arm around Dad. "I can't go out looking like this. This T-shirt smells. I was exercising in it."

"That's fashionable, Mom," Chloe said, looking up from her notebook. "You're a woman of the nineties."

Halfway down the stairs, Mom gave us an order. "Please get me a clean sweatshirt now. There's probably one in the dryer."

Chloe and I got the hint. We raced downstairs into the laundry room. I removed the bat that was braced against a brick and keeping the dryer door closed. Dad said our dryer was good for another year. It was just minus one spring.

Chloe grabbed the first large sweatshirt she found and ran back upstairs. I stopped in the kitchen and got some scissors.

After I cut Mom free from her fishline, Dad slid the sweatshirt carefully over Mom's head and arms.

"Thanks," she said. "I feel so much better. I hate calling attention to myself."

Dad and I exchanged looks.

We didn't tell her she was wearing her brother's sweatshirt and that it had a message on the back:

NO WAIT

NO FUSS

GAS UP

WITH GUS

Uncle Gus has a habit of dropping by the house for dinner and leaving his laundry.

Dad made a quick call to Uncle Gus. He wanted to make sure he was coming over tonight. He told Gus he and Mom might be several hours at the hospital.

"So, Derrick and I can't check out the action at the emergency room?" I said, closing the car door.

Dad shook his head. "You two hold the fort until Gus gets here. Chloe isn't old enough to be by herself late at night. You can camp out later. Play a game of Scrabble with your sister. She likes word games."

Word games?

That wasn't exactly how Derrick and I planned to spend our evening.

We were supposed to be counting stars and watching for the Shadow.

After they drove off, the three of us went into the living room and got out a board game.

Derrick wasn't happy about it, but he got a smile on his face for some reason.

"Hey, I just remembered I brought something for us." He took off his jacket and hung it up carefully in the hall closet. After he unbuttoned his vest, he reached inside the pocket and took out a giant pack of gum. The kind with twenty sticks.

"All right!" I said. I liked the idea of putting a fat gum wad in my mouth and grossing out Chloe.

After Derrick pulled the string around the yellow wrapper, he took out one stick and broke it in two pieces.

I looked at my half stick, and shook my head. I was thinking of a big wad.

All I got was a tightwad.

7

The FBI and CIA Clash

About thirty seconds later I spit out my gum. The flavor was long gone.

While Chloe set up the Scrabble board, I poured some apple juice into three glasses, and Derrick emptied trail mix into a bowl. As he looked at the raisins, peanuts, dried apricots, sunflower seeds, and banana chips, he shook his head. "Don't you have any real snacks at your house?"

"It's a bummer," I said. "Mom started a new diet last week. Remember? She's really concerned about how she looks lately."

Then I thought about Greg Parks again.

Derrick could tell my mind wasn't on the Scrabble game. He kept cracking dumb jokes to make me laugh, but it didn't work. I just sat there with a long face.

For one half hour, we took turns making words on the Scrabble board. You could tell who made which word.

DOUGH.

BANK.

FILM.

Those were Derrick's words.

IDIOT.

CREEPS.

NITWIT.

Those were Chloe's. I could tell she didn't care for our company.

MAN.

MOTHER.

PAIN.

Those were mine. I had the letter tiles for GREG, but in Scrabble you can't use proper names.

Halfway through the game, Chloe drew an "S" tile and made "Idiot" plural.

"Just like your FBI," she snipped.

Derrick winked at me. "You mean . . . Fat Booger-eating Idiots? Orp and I loved your sign."

Chloe looked down at the floor.

"Don't be embarrassed," Derrick said. "We like the title you made up, don't we, Orp?"

I broke out into a smile. Derrick was putting her on.

"In fact, we love boogers. We're going to eat some right now. Want to watch?"

"STOP!"

When Chloe covered her eyes, Derrick reached into the trail mix bowl and pressed one raisin on his index finger. After he made some phony munching noises, he said, "Mmmmmmm, that was delicious. I have to have another one."

Chloe slowly took her hands away from her eyes. When she saw Derrick's finger, she immediately stood up. "That's the biggest booger I've ever seen. Derrick Jones, you're disgusting! I'm leaving."

"But I picked this one for you," Derrick said. And he got up and started walking slowly toward Chloe.

"ORP!" Chloe yelled. "Help!"

When Uncle Gus arrived at 10:55, Derrick was chasing Chloe all over the house.

"HELP!" Chloe screamed. "DERRICK HAS A BOOGER."

Uncle Gus smiled. "Ahhhhhh, home, sweet home." Then he paused. "Okay you clowns, listen up. I just heard a bulletin on my truck radio."

Chloe and Derrick stopped running.

"What?" they replied.

"Boston Bull was sighted at St. Mary's Hospital."

"St. Mary's!" I said. "That's where Mom is!"

We all made a beeline to the TV.

8

Mom's on TV!

As soon as I found the needlenose pliers, I turned on the TV.

The eleven o'clock news was just coming on as we gathered around the TV set.

A reporter stood in front of the hospital with a microphone and camera crew.

"Good evening. We are coming to you live here at St. Mary's Hospital in Hartford, talking with Dr. Goldberg. . . ."

"DR. GOLDBERG!" I said. "We know him!"

"Shhhh!" Chloe replied.

"Did you see Boston Bull?" the reporter asked.

"Well, I didn't know it was him at the time. I was removing a fishhook from a patient and . . ."

"FISHHOOK!" we screamed.

"Go on, Doctor," the reporter replied.

"Well . . . this guy came barging in asking to be bandaged up. He had a deep cut on his right shoulder. Looked like it was ripped by barbed wire and getting infected."

"What did you do?" the reporter asked.

"I washed his wound, applied some antiseptics, and put bandages on him. Since he was armed and dangerous, I just did what he said."

"How did he get in the emergency room where you were?"

"He posed as a delivery boy for Heavenly Pizza. He was carrying a pizza box and the secretary at the front desk thought he was delivering it to the staff."

"How soon were you able to alert the police?"

"As soon as he ran out the automatic door. Minutes later, there must have been a dozen squad cars."

We watched the reporter step into the corridor to a crowd of people.

"Here's another witness at the St. Mary's Emergency Ward. I'll just ask her to turn around for a moment. May I have your name, please?"

"MOM!" we shouted.

"Margie Pygenski."

Uncle Gus jumped off the couch and put his thumbs up. "She's got my sweatshirt on! NO WAIT NO FUSS GAS UP WITH GUS. All right! Free advertisement on TV!"

"Shhhh!" we all said.

"You were the one who got a fishhook in your back?" the reporter asked.

Mom covered her face.

"Turn around again, Margie," Uncle Gus whispered.

"SHHHH!" Chloe jabbed him one.

"Tell me, Ms. Pygenski, were you afraid when you saw Boston Bull?"

"I didn't know it was him. He said he was delivering a pizza. It smelled like sausage. He had a box in his arms."

The reporter turned and pointed the microphone to the doctor. "Do you care to add anything, Dr. Goldberg?"

"Yes. I'm very thankful no one got hurt and that the police came as quickly as they did."

"Thank you, Dr. Goldberg. Oh, by the way, did you find out if it was a real pizza?"

"Yes, I did. It was sausage."

"How did you know?"

"He left me a piece."

The reporter smiled. "This is Bill Vasquez from St. Mary's Hospital. Back to you, Sally."

Derrick and I stood up. "We missed all the action," I groaned.

Then suddenly there was a loud banging noise in front of our house.

Gus dashed to the window and pulled back the drapes. All of us could see the flashing red lights. "You want action? We've got it! A police car just pulled up."

"BOSTON BULL IS IN THE NEIGHBORHOOD!" Derrick yelled. "IT'S A SHOOT-OUT! EVERYBODY DUCK!"

9

An Unexpected Visitor

We all watched Derrick run to the hall closet, step inside, and close the door.

It wasn't his finest hour.

Chloe took the first shot. "Your FBI partner is sure tough, Orvie."

"Hold your fire, Chloe," Uncle Gus replied. "For all you know, we may wind up in there with him."

When we heard another two bangs, Chloe and Ralph ducked inside the closet, too.

"Move over!" Chloe said to Derrick.

I stepped behind Uncle Gus. I didn't want him to see my teeth chattering. This was a scary moment.

Two minutes later, someone came up our steps. Uncle Gus opened the door right away. He knew our doorbell didn't work.

There on the lighted porch was a tall policewoman. She had dark, shoulder-length hair and cool-green eyes. They reminded me of the lime sherbet we'd had for dessert.

I opened the closet door. I wanted Derrick to see what he was running away from.

"Good evening," the policewoman said. "I'm Sergeant Smith. Are you okay?"

Uncle Gus looked confused. "Yes . . . why? Won't you please come in?"

As soon as the policewoman stepped inside, she took off her cap. "Someone has been trying to call you all evening."

"No kidding?" Uncle Gus replied.

Boy, was I relieved! This was just a routine visit.

"I'll check the phone," I said. When I returned from the kitchen, I had the answer. "It was off the hook. Dad didn't put it back after he talked with you, Uncle Gus."

"That happens," Sergeant Smith said. "You probably didn't hear the warning signal. It doesn't last very long."

Uncle Gus nodded. "We make a lot of noise at this house."

Sergeant Smith smiled. "So does my patrol car!"

Derrick and Chloe finally stepped out of the closet. "Is that what those bangs were?" Derrick asked.

Sergeant Smith laughed. "Yes! My muffler just snapped. I've got to get it fixed right away."

"Maybe I could help," Uncle Gus said. "I repair cars every day. I don't have my tools here, but I've fixed lots of mufflers with a coat hanger."

"Really?" Sergeant Smith said.

"Really."

When the two exchanged smiles, it was like watching two batteries getting charged. Even Derrick felt the sparks. He reached in the closet and handed Uncle Gus a hanger.

Chloe didn't pick up on the possible romance. She was all business. "What are those different compartments on your belt?"

Uncle Gus looked at the sergeant's waist. Then her lime-sherbet eyes.

Was Trang in trouble? I wondered.

"This one is for my flashlight. This one is for my latex gloves."

"Gloves?" Chloe replied.

"In case I have to touch any body fluids. It's for my protection and others'. This one is for handcuffs. This is for my portable radio . . ."

When the phone rang, Uncle Gus, Chloe, and Derrick didn't budge. It was left to me.

I walked into the kitchen and got it. "Hello?"

"Orp?"

"Dad! How's Mom?"

"She's going to be fine. How are you?"

"Fine."

"That's good. Everyone in the emergency room is talking about Boston Bull, and your mom has been worried sick about you. She was convinced Boston Bull escaped to our neighborhood, broke into our house, and knocked over the phone."

"No. It was just you, Dad. Remember when you called Uncle Gus? You didn't put the receiver back."

"Oh, geez! I guess there's more than one klutz in our house."

I laughed.

"So Dad, tell me about Boston Bull."

"I will later. There's a line at this phone. Did Gus get there?"

"Yeah."

"Good. Okay, we'll be home in about an hour."

"Okay, Dad. Bye."

After I hung up and returned to the living room, Chloe was still asking questions. "So what do the two stripes mean on your shoulder?"

"Each one stands for five years of service."

When she put her police hat back on, I noticed she wasn't wearing any rings. She was probably about Uncle Gus's age and single, too.

It didn't seem like Trang had to worry about any competition, though. There has been a long tradition of weird names in our family. Smith wasn't odd enough. I decided to check, though, just in case.

"May I ask your first name?"

Uncle Gus's ears seemed to enlarge when I asked that question.

"Penelope. But everyone calls me Pen."

Chloe took out her notebook. "I love that name!"

Uh-oh, I thought. Trang *was* in trouble. If Gus

ever got together with that sergeant and married her, she'd be Pen Stasion.

That fit with our family.

As soon as Uncle Gus walked Pen out the door, Derrick rushed over to the window and peeked behind the curtains. "This is better than Clark Gable and Claudette Colbert in that 1934 classic *It Happened One Night!*"

Derrick was in his glory. It was almost as if he were making his own romantic movie.

Ten minutes later, Gus returned to the house. "The wire surgery is finished!"

"She must have appreciated that," I said.

"Yeah," Uncle Gus said.

Then he broke out into a big smile. "She's going to make me a chocolate-chip pie."

"Ooooooooooh," Derrick and I ooohed.

Uncle Gus laughed.

When Chloe showed up again in the living room, we could tell Pen Smith had an effect on her, too.

We looked down at Chloe's waist. There were six items tucked under her jeans belt:

A flashlight.

A washcloth.

Garden gloves.

Twine.

A notebook.

A pen.

"The CIA is ready for a Kushman stakeout now."

Derrick and I cracked up.

"Fine," I said. "Just don't get in the way of our FBI operation."

10

It Happened After Midnight

Derrick and I headed on outside to our tent while Uncle Gus and Chloe started a new game of Scrabble. I grabbed an extra blanket off my bed.

Derrick grabbed two.

The night air was crisp and the temperature was dropping below 50°.

Derrick and I got undressed in the dark. He folded his tie, vest, suspenders, and white shirt in a neat pile and placed his hat on top.

"No Sam Spade pajamas?" I asked.

"Are you kidding?" Derrick replied. "Sam Spade would have slept in his underwear."

I smiled. He didn't notice I was in my underwear, too.

Once we got inside our sleeping bags, it was comfortable. We each had a flashlight so we could check for any prowlers.

So far there were two.

One was a daddy longlegs walking over my arm.

The other was Ralph. He was swishing his tail in my face.

Nothing that Sam Spade would be concerned with. But Derrick and I had to check them out anyway.

We zipped the tent door and unzipped the tent window flap so we could stake out the side window of the Kushman living room.

"You know, Derrick, watching for the Shadow is like fishing."

"How's that?"

"Well, when you're fishing, you sit there, watch that red bobber, and wait for some fish to suck it under the water. Here, you watch that side window and wait for a dim light. If it comes on, you and I get sucked out of this tent."

"Great analogy, Orp. But what's the bait that attracts the Shadow?"

"If we knew that, we'd probably know who the Shadow was. I mean why *would* someone want to be in the Kushman living room? And why be so secretive about it?"

"Good questions," Derrick said.

Suddenly car lights shined in our driveway. I could hear the car doors slam, and my parents talking as they walked over to the tent.

"Hit the hay!" I whispered to Derrick. "Mom has probably changed her mind about our sleeping out tonight."

Derrick immediately started snoring.

I lay perfectly still on my back like a corpse.

"Orp?" Dad called. "Are you boys okay?"

They unzipped the tent and looked in. Mom had a flashlight and shined it in our faces.

"Let's wake them up," Mom said, "and get them inside."

"They're fine, Margie," Dad replied. "They're sound asleep. Our bedroom looks out on the backyard. They're warm enough. Look at all their blankets. And they've got a bodyguard."

"What bodyguard?" Mom asked.

"Ralph. He's sleeping right between them. He'll ward off Boston Bull."

Mom didn't laugh.

"Come on, Margie. Let's go to bed. We've had enough excitement to last us for a while."

As soon as they zipped up the tent flap and walked back to the house, I whispered, "Derrick?"

When there was no answer, I looked over at him. Derrick was fast asleep! His arm was around Ralph.

The stakeout was left to me!

For fifteen long minutes, I kept staring at the tent window.

And counting stars.

When I was on ninety-three . . . it happened!

A very faint light came up the front porch stairs.

A door opened and closed.

And then the dim light went on in the living room.

"DERRICK!" I whispered as loud as I could. "HE'S HERE!"

Derrick popped up like a jack-in-the-box. "What? Who?"

"THE SHADOW!" I said.

Derrick took a quick look out the tent window. "It's HIM!"

"You've got it!" I said, pulling on my jeans and jacket. "We can't see the Shadow from here. Let's get going!"

I noted the time. "It's twelve forty-five A.M.! That's unusual for the Eight o'Clock Shadow."

"Or B-B-Boston Bull," Derrick stuttered as he tied his right sneaker.

"Hurry!" I said.

"I can't find my left sneaker."

"Come on, Derrick! You're just stalling!"

Derrick stood up in the center of the tent. "I am *not* stalling. I jumped into my jeans and put my jacket over my T-shirt. You're looking at one tough detective. I'm going outside with one bare foot in forty-nine-degree weather and I won't squawk about it."

Derrick made it sound like he was one of George Washington's men crossing the Delaware.

"All right!" I said, flicking on my flashlight. "It's Shadow time!"

11
Shadow Time

Quickly I tiptoed down the driveway to the Kushman living-room window.

Derrick hobbled behind me.

When we got to the cedar bush, we crouched down and watched.

"Man!" Derrick said. "This is better than that 1954 Alfred Hitchcock movie, *Rear Window.*"

"Oooooooh!" I said. "Look at that! The Shadow is moving back and forth."

"Wait! He stopped now," Derrick whispered.

"What's he doing?" I asked.

When I heard faint rustling behind us, I immediately turned around. It was Ralph. I knew what he was doing.

"Orp!" Derrick said, pulling on my jacket. "He's making a bomb! I'm sure of it. Look at that thing on the table. He's building something."

"What do you think it is?" I whispered.

"It's a bomb, I tell you!" Derrick repeated.

For fifteen minutes we watched the Shadow build that mysterious object with his hands.

"He just added another piece," I said. "Look how big it is now!"

Suddenly, the dim light went out and everything turned black in the house. Derrick and I didn't move one inch.

The back door opened and closed.

"He has to come around to the front," Derrick whispered. "If . . . he comes this way, he might see us."

"There isn't much light," I said. "Just a little from that street-corner lamp. Squat some more!"

"M-m-maybe th-the Shadow went the other way," Derrick hoped.

"There's a p-p-pickup . . . truck parked at the corner."

Now I was stuttering.

Sweat dripped from my pits to my waist.

Stalking the Shadow in the middle of the night was a lot scarier than at eight o'clock.

Suddenly I felt a gloved hand around my neck.

"Aaaaaaaaauuuuuugh!" I gasped.

Derrick jumped out of the cedar bush. "AAAAAAAAAAUUUUUGH!"

We both looked at our attacker in terror!

"CHLOE!"

"I was watching the whole operation from my bedroom window. Did you see where the Shadow went?"

My heart was racing so fast, I couldn't talk.

Derrick did for me. "DON'T *EVER* SNEAK UP ON US LIKE THAT AGAIN! Man, you gave us both heart attacks!"

"I was just giving my handsome brother a goodnight hug."

"Funny," I grumbled. I stepped away from the bushes. "Do you think the Shadow's gone?"

"There's no sign of him," Derrick said as he checked the driveway.

"Eweyee!" he whispered. "I just stepped in something."

Derrick wiped his bare foot on the grass.

When I flashed my light on his foot, we all saw the brown guck.

"Geez," Derrick complained. "Cold dog doo."

Chloe unbuttoned her jacket and pulled out her washrag that was tucked in her belt. "Come over by the hose, Derrick. The CIA will take care of you."

Derrick didn't say thanks. He was still angry about her scaring us.

"Tomorrow," I said, "we'll be wiser. When it's eight o'clock, the FBI will cover both doors! We won't let him get away next time."

Chloe looked up from her water surgery. She was still wearing her garden gloves. No doubt this time to protect her from Ralph's body fluids.

"The CIA will back you guys up," Chloe announced.

Just as I started to object, Derrick held up a hand. "I don't want her sneaking up on us again, Orp. Let her join us this *one time.*"

I thought about it.

My sister had weaseled her way into the biggest operation of our FBI.

"Once," I grumbled. "Just this once."

12

A New Clue— Jenny Lee's Letter

The next morning the sun felt warm shining through our tent. Mom was standing over us with some mail in one hand, and a spatula in the other.

"There's blueberry pancakes if you boys are hungry," she said.

I sat up and looked at Mom. She was smiling. "How come you're in such a good mood?"

"I never knew what a blessing it was not to have a fishhook in your back."

"Or a bullet in your side," Derrick added. "You were awfully close to Boston Bull, Mrs. Pygenski."

Mom sighed. "Right. I'm so thankful to be alive and well after last night's ordeal. No more complaining from me."

I got out of my sleeping bag. "I wonder if Uncle Gus will have a booming oil and lube business today after all that free advertisement."

Mom laughed. "I guess I was a walking billboard."

"Any mail for me?" I asked.

"Eh . . . let's see," Mom said, flipping through the pile. "Do you know anyone from Ohio, Orp?"

"JENNY LEE!" I said, snatching the letter. Then I remembered Derrick gazing over my shoulder. No one knew I called her that. "Hmmm . . . a letter from my pen pal, Jennifer. You might as well go have some pancakes, Derrick. I'll be there in a minute."

"You're not fooling me, Orp," Derrick replied while he pulled on his jeans. "Everyone knows Jennifer's your girlfriend."

"OUT!" I shouted.

Mom just laughed.

After they left, I zipped up the tent and let Ralph position his paws on my chest and his black nose in my face.

He and I kind of have the habit of reading Jenny Lee's letters together.

As soon as I opened the letter, I counted the hearts in the border. Twenty-five this time.

Ralph opened his mouth and panted.

My feelings exactly, I thought.

I was sure glad that Jenny Lee's parents and my parents went to high school together. That's how we met. Her parents came to visit mine last summer as kind of a reunion.

I'll never forget that first moment I saw Jenny Lee through the crack of the kitchen door. Those YMCA-pool-blue eyes and Dorothy Hamill hairdo.

Slowly, I began reading the letter:

Dear Orville,

You must be on spring break now. Isn't it great! My softball team is practicing two and a half hours a day, so I'm getting a workout at first base.

I wish I could see you pitch in one of your Cornell games. But I'm not the one who gets to travel. My parents do! They're going to Eaton, Ohio, Saturday for their 25th high school reunion. Are your parents going? It would be great if they could all get together again.

Suddenly I put the letter down. Mom hadn't mentioned her reunion at all. Did Dad know about it?

Was that why she was looking at her yearbook?

I had to finish the letter. Detective work usually comes first with me. But . . . in this case, it was after Jenny Lee.

I can't wait for you to
come to Ohio in July to
visit. There's lots of
things we can do

Swim.

Fish.

Play basketball and baseball.

And just be together.

I miss you.

Love,

Jenny Lee

P.S.
It's my turn to call. Talk to you Friday
night at seven.

13

One Case Solved!

When I got back in the house, Mom was serving seconds to Chloe and Derrick.

"So what's new, loverboy?" Derrick asked before he guzzled down some orange juice.

I ignored him, sat down, and stared at the stack of pancakes on my plate.

"How's Jennifer?" Chloe asked.

"Fine." There was no way I was going to share the intimate details of my life with them.

Mom's life? That was different. It was time for

a direct hit. "I didn't know your high school class was having a reunion, Mom."

Mom turned around from the stove. "How did you know?"

"Jennifer told me her parents are going."

Derrick and Chloe looked up. We were all thinking the same thing. Was this related somehow to the Mysterious Letter and Case #2?

Mom sat down at the kitchen table. "I was going to tell you later when your dad got home from work, but I might as well tell you now. We are driving out to Ohio for our twenty-fifth high school reunion. Uncle Gus said he'd stay with you while we're gone."

"You *are* going?" I asked.

Mom nodded. "I . . . got the invitation a while ago, and dragged my feet. I was feeling . . . fat and ugly and didn't think I wanted to go. But after that life-threatening ordeal last night, I realized how petty I've been. It's time to celebrate! Take a trip and enjoy life!"

Then Mom added, "Even if I am chubs."

"You're not chubs, Mom," Chloe said.

"Is there going to be fishing?" I asked.

"Yes. Our class chartered a boat on the Ohio River. There will be dinner, dancing, and fishing."

"I thought so," Chloe said. "That explains your fly-fishing in the attic."

Mom shook her head. "Yes."

"So who's Greg Parks?" Derrick blurted out.

Chloe and I froze. We couldn't believe Derrick asked the question.

"He was President of our Senior Class. He sent out the invitations. How'd you know his name?"

Chloe pushed her dish away. "We . . . I found his envelope in our garbage. I never saw the letter, Mom. I wouldn't invade your privacy."

Now it was time for *my* confession. "Mom . . . when Derrick and I were in the attic yesterday, we . . . we read what Greg Parks wrote in your yearbook. I'm sorry we were being so nosy."

Chloe's eyes bulged. She didn't know about our discovery.

Mom shook her head. "Oh that? Don't worry about it! I found out later Greg wrote the same thing in a lot of girls' yearbooks. He flattered us all. That's how he got so many votes for President."

"Ohhhhhhh," Derrick and I replied. Boy was I relieved that the ol' love triangle melted away like butter on a stove.

Suddenly my stack of pancakes looked awfully good. I picked up my fork and chowed down!

Twenty minutes later, Derrick and I walked back outside to the tent. Chloe followed us like a barking hound. "You guys should not have revealed our sources of information. Good detectives don't do that."

Derrick rolled his eyes at me.

Quickly, we ducked inside the tent. When Chloe tried to join us, I zipped the tent door in her face.

"Sorry," I said. "FBI only. This is off-limits for your CIA. We agreed to combine agencies for our stakeout only. Meet you at the cedar bush at seven fifty-five."

Then I checked my watch. "In about . . . nine hours, we'll find out just *who* the Shadow is!"

"Well . . . " Chloe grumbled, "I know *who* you two are!" "Fat Boog . . ."

"BATHTUB INVESTIGATORS!" Derrick and I shouted. We drowned out Chloe perfectly.

That was a three pointer!

14

Stalking the Shadow

At 7:56 we were hiding in the bushes, waiting for the dim light to come on.

"The guy is like clockwork," Derrick whispered. "I've got three and a half minutes till eight on my watch."

"What time do you have?" I asked Chloe.

She checked her luminous watch. "Seven fifty-eight."

Quickly I briefed Chloe on her position. "As soon as the Shadow turns off the light, you and Derrick run to the back door. I'm taking the front."

"How come I'm backing up Derrick and not you?" Chloe asked.

"Because he didn't mind if you were his backup. I did."

"Thanks," Chloe said.

"You're welcome," I replied.

At 8:00, the dim light came on.

"Look! There's the Shadow!" Chloe said.

"Oooooh, neato!" Derrick replied.

"I'm convinced he's got a key," I said. "He slips in and out of that house like a . . . *slippery* shadow! Well, he won't slip by us tonight!"

"Step back," Chloe said. "You can see better."

Quietly we moved back from the bush. What a perfect view! The Shadow was moving up and down now.

Kicking.

Bending.

Punching.

What was he doing?

We watched for thirty minutes. At exactly 8:30 P.M. the light went out.

"Man your stations!" I called.

Chloe and Derrick ran to the back door, and I ran to the front.

Now, both porches were covered. I ducked down behind the bushes and waited.

I could hear Chloe telling Derrick to hold the other end of her twine. She was planning to trip the Shadow!

I squatted. Then I heard it.

A door opening and closing.

It was the Kushmans' front door.

The one I was guarding!

My body started shaking. Sweat rolled down my armpits and forehead. I was almost too afraid to look. What if he saw me?

What if the Shadow *did* turn out to be Boston Bull? Would I be full of holes?

Lying on the ground.

Dead.

At the age of twelve going on thirteen.

Reason slowly entered my brain. It was dark. The Shadow wouldn't know I was there. He wouldn't look over. And I was a detective. Sam Spade took risks. I had to take mine.

After all, this was a stakeout.

As soon as I heard footsteps going down the front steps, I raised my head and looked.

Oh . . . no!

It couldn't be.

My body froze! I was so stunned.

A minute later, when the Shadow was gone, Derrick and Chloe came running over to me.

"Did you see him?"

I nodded slowly.

"Are you okay, Orp?" Chloe asked.

I nodded again.

"Was it . . . Boston Bull?" Derrick quizzed.

I shook my head.

"Where did he go?" they asked.

I turned and pointed.

"Not our house," Chloe said.

"Yes . . ."

15
The Shadow Confesses

As soon as we got in the house, Dad told us about the 8:00 news flash on TV. "They caught Boston Bull two hours ago. He was found dozing in an inner tube floating down the Connecticut River."

Then Dad added, "They also found an empty Heavenly Pizza box at his side."

We didn't ask any questions. We just plopped down on the couch.

I had my own news flash.

The identity of the Shadow.

"Who was it?" Derrick begged.

"Tell us!" Chloe pleaded.

I looked at Dad.

"Where does Mom go every night at eight?" I asked.

Dad looked dazed. "Well, lately she's been running errands."

Derrick and Chloe leaned back.

"It was Mom?" Chloe looked dumbfounded.

"What are you talking about?" Mom said as she strolled into the living room, wearing a sweatshirt and sweatpants.

"Why do you go to the Kushmans' house every night at eight?" I asked.

Mom took a step back. "How did you know that?"

"We've been watching your shadow through the Kushmans' living-room window."

Mom covered her face with her hands. "And I thought I had complete privacy!"

We all leaned forward as Mom continued her explanation. "Okay, I . . . wanted to watch the *Stretch with Fletch Show* on TV. I know your Dad likes the news. I thought I could work a bit on my figure before our class reunion. The Kushmans gave me a key to check on things, water their plants, and feed their goldfish. I didn't think they would mind."

"Why didn't you tell us?" I asked.

"I thought you'd make fun of my exercising or want to come over and watch. It just seemed easier to do it on my own. Privately."

Chloe smiled. "I like to do some things privately, too, Mom. Like write my novels."

Mom smiled back. "I'm sorry if I worried you. It was only thirty minutes."

"What caused that big noise last night around eight fifteen P.M. at the Kushmans'?" Derrick asked.

Mom lowered her eyes. "You know what a klutz I can be sometimes. . . ."

No one said anything, but we all knew it was true.

"Well, I was doing a kicking exercise and knocked over their big vase. Fortunately, I was able to glue it together until I can buy them another one."

"Is that what you were doing in the middle of the night?" I asked. "Gluing the vase?"

"Yes. I couldn't sleep. That was after we got back late from the emergency room. Just leaving the broken pieces bothered me. And, it was something to do. I needed more time to wind down. The evening was very upsetting."

"How come I didn't know about that trip next door?" Dad asked.

"You were snoring, Orville. There was no need to wake you."

"So . . ." Derrick said, "that was what the sculpture show was all about. You were gluing lamp pieces back together."

Mom nodded.

"That's it!" I said. "Now we have all the missing pieces of the Shadow case. You gave us some exciting moments, Mom. For a while, we thought you were Boston Bull hiding out."

Dad chuckled. "You were close! It turned out to be the Hartford Heifer!"

When Mom got Dad in an armlock, he didn't try to get free. He just laughed.

Chloe stood up, took out her journal, and made her grand exit. "This whole evening has inspired me to write another chapter in my new book!"

Derrick turned and slapped me five. "What do you say, Orp, I still have an hour left before

Mom picks me up. Want to play a little Monopoly?"

"Well, Derrick, now that we're seasoned detectives, how about a game of Clue?"

"You're on, Schweetheart!"

Epilogue

Friday night I sat comfortably in my office, my feet on the faucet handles and the phone in my hand.

It was 6:55 P.M.

Mom and Dad were in Ohio by now. Uncle Gus was making quesadillas in the kitchen. Pen was coming over any minute with the dessert.

Chocolate-chip pie.

I wondered what Trang would think of that. She was returning from a business trip on Sunday.

Uncle Gus warned me once about having two

girlfriends. I think he's heading toward one big explosion.

I wasn't adding *that* romantic mystery to my list, though. Some cases only time can tell. Like Derrick's Sam Spade act. Would he get booed? I'd just have to wait and see.

Chloe barged in without knocking. "I knew you were in your think tank again. Do you mind if I floss?"

"Go right ahead. Where did you find it?"

Chloe reached down and pet Ralph, who was asleep next to the tub. "He found it under the bathroom rug."

"That's it, then. Except for the TV knob, most of the mysteries around the house are solved. I found the green basketball on the garage roof, Ralph's dog dish behind the refrigerator, and Mom's cat earring turned up in the Kushmans' mailbox."

Chloe flicked a piece of ham out of her teeth. I could smell it from the tub.

"I hope you're through," I said.

Chloe ignored my wish.

"Didn't you forget your gym socks?" Chloe replied as she returned the cinnamon dental floss to the medicine cabinet. "You said they were missing, too."

"Oh, I don't care about them."

"Good," Chloe said. "Because I used them for a sock puppet project two weeks ago. They make great heads."

"Thanks a lot!" Chloe was bugging me now. Why was she hanging around? "Don't you have a mystery novel to finish?"

"I'm on Chapter Three. Just taking a break. Want to hear a few pages?"

"Not now!" I said. "I'm expecting a business call any minute."

"Sure you are. Dream on."

When the phone rang seconds later, Chloe took a step back.

"Excuse me," I said.

Chloe slammed the bathroom door.

Ahhhh, victory was never sweeter.

After the second ring, I picked up the receiver. "Hello?"

"Or . . . Orville?"

"Jenny Lee! How are you?"

"I . . ."

Her voice sounded upset.

"What's the matter?"

"I'm . . . worried about Mom. You know she and Dad left this morning to go to their reunion tomorrow. . . ."

"Right. . . ."

"Well, I got out her senior yearbook and read some of the things her classmates wrote. . . ."

"Uh-huh. . . ."

"And I think . . . she may be meeting someone else there."

"Are you talking about the possibility of a love triangle?"

"Yes. . . ."

I smiled.

"I know it sounds funny, Orville, but Mom got this letter from a Greg Parks, and he wrote in her yearbook that she made him . . ."

". . . melt like butter?"

"Oh, Orville . . . how did you know?"

After her sweet voice made my toes curl, I began my explanation. "Jenny Lee, let me tell you about my FBI work this week. . . ."

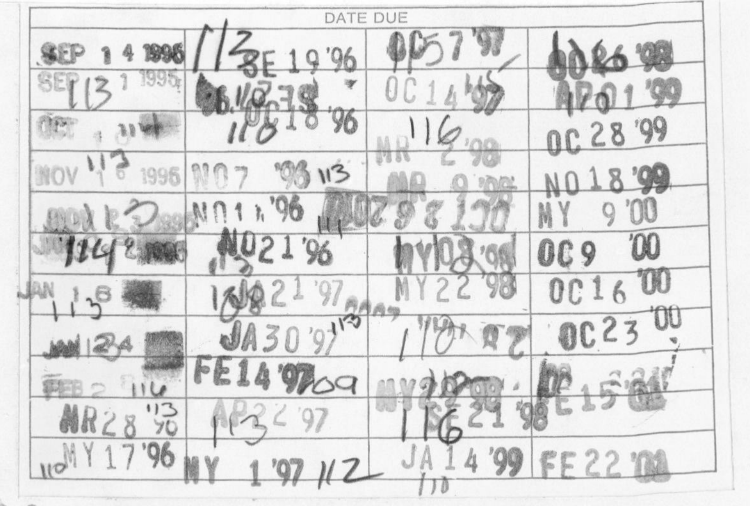

Kline, Suzy

Orp and the FBI